Grim, Grunt and Grizzle-Tail

For Eleanor and
Joel, with love — F. P.

To my dear brother,
Pierre — S. F.

Barefoot Books
2067 Massachusetts Ave
Cambridge, MA 02140

Barefoot Books
29/30 Fitzroy Square
London, W1T 6LQ

First published in the United States of America by Barefoot Books, Inc
and in Great Britain by Barefoot Books, Ltd in 2013
This paperback edition first published in 2020. All rights reserved

Graphic design by Judy Linard, London, England
Reproduction by B & P International, Hong Kong
Printed in China on 100% acid-free paper
This book was typeset in Khaki, Sassoon Primary and Mr Anteater
The illustrations were prepared in acrylics

Thank you to the pupils of Cutteslowe Primary School, Oxford, UK
for all their careful reading

Sources:
Arguedas, Jose Maria, ed. *The Singing Mountaineers: Songs and Tales
of the Quechua People*. University of Texas Press, Austin, 1957.

Payne, Johnny, ed. *The She-Calf and Other Quechua Folk Tales*.
University of New Mexico Press, Albuquerque, 2000.

Pino-Saavedra, Yolando, ed. *Folktales of Chile*.
Routledge & Kegan Paul, London, 1968.

ISBN 978-1-78285-846-1

British Cataloguing-in-Publication Data: a catalogue
record for this book is available from the British Library

Library of Congress Cataloging-in-Publication Data
is available under LCCN 2012037364

1 3 5 7 9 8 6 4 2

Grim, Grunt and Grizzle-Tail

A Tale from Chile

Retold by Fran Parnell

Illustrated by Sophie Fatus

Barefoot Books
step inside a story

Contents

CHAPTER 1

The Orange Princesses

Long ago and far away, there lived a king. His people loved him, his palace was filled with gold and his corn grew ripe in the hot summer sun.

But, oh my goodness! What was he to do with his three naughty daughters? All day long, they played naughty tricks.

Follow me!

They tied the llamas' tails together. They hid crickets in the king's bed. And they never stopped teasing Pedro, the boy who did all the hard work around the palace. They hid his broom, they stole his shoes and left muddy handprints on the palace wall.

One day, the king lost his temper.
"You're just too bad!" he cried. "I shall
turn you into oranges for a year and a day."

And — pling! — it was done. The girls had gone. Instead, three beautiful golden oranges hung from the orange tree in the palace garden. The king put a guard under the tree to make sure that his daughters were safe.

I'm so important.

For a long time, the palace was very peaceful and all was well.

But the story of the three orange princesses passed in whispers from mouth to ear. It got louder and louder, until at last, deep underground, in the Land of Monsters, the creatures who lived there heard it too.

In that land lived three brothers called Grim, Grunt and Grizzle-Tail. The brothers were as horrible as their names. Each one had the head of an enormous bull.

Sharp white tusks poked from their mouths. Their long tails were angry snakes that lashed and thrashed. Scaly wings flapped on their backs. And they could run faster than the wind on their puma feet.

The eldest brother, Grim, shouted,
"I want an orange princess! Go and get
one for me, shorty." He gave his littlest
brother a push and a shove. With a sigh,
Grizzle-Tail sprang on his puma feet into
the world above.

Get a move
on, shorty!

CHAPTER 2

A Fright in the Night

Under the orange tree, the guard was yawning. "It's so boring, guarding these oranges night and day," he muttered. "I wish something exciting would happen."

Be careful what you wish for. There was a flapping of scaly wings and a horrible roar, then out of the night flew Grizzle-Tail. The guard ran screaming for the hills. Grizzle-Tail reached out a clawed paw and snatched the nearest orange. Then off he flew, back home to the Land of Monsters.

The king was very upset. He offered
a reward to anyone who could find his
stolen daughter and he sent another man
to guard the tree.

Back in the Land of Monsters, Grim was happy with his princess, but Grunt was jealous. "I want an orange princess too!" he bellowed. "Go and get one for me, baby-face." And he gave his littlest brother a push.

I love my orange...

With a roll of his eyes, Grizzle-Tail leapt up into the world above on his puma feet.

Under the orange tree, the second guard was huffing and puffing. "I'm so bored!" he groaned. "I wish something exciting would happen."

I'm bored.

Wishes can be dangerous. There was
a flapping of scaly wings and a horrible
roar, then out of the night flew Grizzle-Tail.

Yelling in terror, the guard raced away
down the road. Grizzle-Tail reached out a
clawed paw, snatched a second orange,
soared high into the sky and flew home
with his prize.

The next morning, fat, wet tears rolled down the king's cheeks. He offered a bigger reward, but nobody knew where his stolen daughters were. No one wanted to guard the tree anymore, either — it was far too frightening.

Now, Pedro missed the princesses too. They had teased him, but the palace was too quiet without their noise and chatter and naughty tricks. He stood up strong and tall and went to the king.

"I will look after the orange tree," Pedro said in his bravest voice.

"You can try if you like," said the king. "Here is a sword. Guard the tree carefully, because if my last daughter is also stolen, I will throw you in the dungeon."

I'll do my best.

CHAPTER 3

The Monster's Trail

Grim and Grunt were happy with their beautiful fruit. "You must have an orange princess too!" they shouted at Grizzle-Tail. "Go and get one!" And they shoved their little brother backwards and forwards, until at last he shouted, "Oh, all RIGHT! I will fetch the last princess." And off he flew.

Under the orange tree, Pedro watched the sun set. He listened hard, held his sword tight and waited. Suddenly, with a horrible roar, Grizzle-Tail flew out of the darkness, his long claws stretching for the last golden orange.

Pedro's heart thumped in his chest, but he jumped up and hit the monster with his sword. "OWWW!" howled Grizzle-Tail. The sword had cut his shoulder. But still he grabbed the last orange and flew away with it into the sky.

Poor Pedro! He had done his best,
but the last orange was gone. He did not
want to be thrown in the dungeon, so
he ran away. Then he noticed something
odd. Here and there, spits and spots, drips
and drops of the monster's blood had
fallen in the road.

Pedro cheered up. "At least I can follow the monster's trail," he thought. "I'll see if I can catch him."

Pedro walked and walked. Soon he bumped into the two guards.

Look! It's Pedro.

"I'm following the monster's trail,"
said Pedro. "Why don't we look for him
together? If we can find the princesses, the
king will reward us all instead of throwing
us in the dungeon."

A greedy look crept over the guards'
faces. They said they would help Pedro,
but secretly they made a plan to get rid of
him and have the reward for themselves.

The trail ended at a great big rock. Under the rock was the deepest, darkest well in the world. The guards' teeth chattered. "We're not going down there!" they whispered.

Pedro looked into the darkness and his head spun like a cartwheel. But he said, "Lower me down, boys. We have to find those princesses."

CHAPTER 4

Into the Well

There was a bucket at the top of the well, with a great loop of rope tied onto the handle. Pedro climbed in and the guards lowered him down into the hole.

"Tug the rope three times when you want us to pull you up," the guards said to Pedro. They gave each other a sneaky look and grinned.

Down, down, down went Pedro. The darkness was so thick, it was hard to breathe. Just as he was about to give up, Pedro saw a tiny light at the bottom.

What a relief! At last, the bucket bumped down onto the ground. Pedro had reached the Land of Monsters.

How deep is this well?

All around were craggy mountains.
Far above was a smudge of blue sky and
standing on the other side of a green
cornfield was a huge castle.

Pedro banged on the castle door.
He took a deep breath and lifted his
sword, ready to fight.

The handle rattled and the door creaked open. There stood the three princesses. A year and a day had passed since the king had first changed them into oranges. The spell had broken.

"Pedro!" said the princesses. "We want to go home. Help us get away from these horrible monsters."

The girls had been playing their old tricks on Grim, Grunt and Grizzle-Tail and the monster brothers were tired out.

Grim and Grunt were fast asleep. It only took a moment for Pedro to tiptoe in and put them to the sword!

But Grizzle-Tail could not sleep. His shoulder still hurt where Pedro's sword had hit him. Pedro stood in front of him, waving his sword and looking fierce. But Grizzle-Tail was not angry. He was very happy to see Pedro.

"Dear Pedro!" he said, throwing his paws around the boy. "You've rid me of my bullying brothers. I never wanted to steal those tricky princesses. Take the girls home and I will be grateful to you forever. And if you ever need my help in return, just shout 'Grizzle-Tail!' three times."

Pedro thought that underneath the claws and tusks and scaly wings, the littlest monster was not so bad.

He took the princesses to the well. They climbed into the bucket and tugged the rope three times and the guards pulled them out of the well.

At last the bucket was ready for Pedro, but just as he was about to climb into it, he heard the guards whisper something. It did not sound kind.

Pedro remembered how greedy they had looked when they were following the monster's trail. He remembered their sneaky looks as he went down into the well. All of a sudden, he felt very worried.

CHAPTER 5

A Horrible
Surprise

Pedro did not climb into the bucket.
Instead, he put a big stone into it and
tugged the rope three times. Then he waited.
Up, up, up went the bucket; but when
it was higher than the treetops, down
it tumbled and CRASH! went the stone,
smashing into a thousand pieces.

Pedro knew that the guards had betrayed him. Now they would take the princesses back to the palace and claim the reward for themselves. He would be stuck at the bottom of this hole forever and never get home again. Pedro was so upset that he lay down and sobbed.

I'll never get home!

Wait! What had he forgotten? Pedro wiped his eyes and blew his nose. The monster had promised to help. Could Pedro trust him? He decided to find out.

"Grizzle-Tail! Grizzle-Tail! GRIZZLE-TAIL!" shouted Pedro.

Before the words were out of Pedro's mouth, Grizzle-Tail was by his side. When he heard the story of the wicked guards, he gave a roar that shook the rocks.

"Climb on my back," he growled. "We will catch them before they get home."

Pedro scrambled onto the monster's
back and with one huge leap Grizzle-Tail
sprang into the world above. He flew
towards the palace, faster than the wind.
The dust billowed and the air howled
while Pedro clung to the monster for
dear life.

They were at the palace gates just in
time! The princesses had stepped inside
and the guards were about to follow. With
a flapping of scaly wings and a horrible
roaring sound, Grizzle-Tail pounced.

CRUNCH! CRUUUNCH! Grizzle-Tail
gobbled up the guards.

Pedro slid off the monster's back
and together they walked into the palace.
Pedro explained how Grizzle-Tail had
helped him and become his friend.

And of course, the king was overjoyed to see his daughters. He hugged them and kissed them.

He rewarded Pedro with gold galore. And he promised never to turn anyone into an orange again.

I love you.